RETRIEVERS

LOYAL HUNTING COMPANIONS

BY TAMMY GAGNE

CONSULTANT:
CHRIS REYNOLDS
MEMBER
AMERICAN HUNTING DOG CLUB

CAPSTONE PRESS
a capstone imprint

Edge Books are published by Capstone Press,
1710 Roe Crest Drive, North Mankato, Minnesota 56003
www.capstonepub.com

Library of Congress Cataloging-in-Publication Data

Gagne, Tammy.
Retrievers : loyal hunting companions / by Tammy Gagne.
p. cm. — (Hunting dogs)
Audience: 8-13.
Audience: Grade 4 to 6.
Includes bibliographical references and index.
Summary: "Describes the history, care, and training of retrievers used for hunting"— Provided by publisher.
ISBN 978-1-4296-9909-9 (library binding)
ISBN 978-1-62065-936-6 (paper over board)
ISBN 978-1-4765-1548-9 (ebook PDF)
1. Retrievers—Juvenile literature. I. Title.
SF429.R4G34 2013
636.752'7—dc23 2012027112

Editorial Credits

Angie Kaelberer, editor; Kyle Grenz, designer; Marcie Spence, media researcher; Jennifer Walker, production specialist

Photo Credits

Alamy Images: Daniel Dempster Photography, 14, 16 (bottom), Kuttig – People, 15, Mark Lisk, 4; Capstone Studio: Karon Dubke, 13, 17, 25; Fiona Green Animal Photography: 5, 20, 21; iStockphoto: LUGO, 1; Newscom: Scott McKiernan, 16 (top); Shutterstock: Alexander Raths, 26, Andresr, 24, artcphotos, 18, Bonita R. Cheshier, cover, eurobanks, 22, Jan S., 27, Joop Snijder, 23 (top), Jorge Salcedo, 9, Kirk Geisler, 28, Linn Currie, 7, Mark Herreid, 23 (bottom), Okeanas, 10, Suzi Nelson, 19, Tatiana Gass, 6, vgm, 12, Zuzule, 8, 11

Printed in the United States of America in Stevens Point, Wisconsin.
092012 006937WZS13

TABLE OF CONTENTS

CHAPTER 1

FETCHING DOGS

As the hunter fires a shot, the duck falls from the sky into the crystal-clear lake. "Fetch!" the hunter says to his retriever. The dog knows just where to find the bird. In minutes, the retriever returns to shore with the mallard in its mouth.

Retrievers are the most popular **sporting dogs**—and for good reason. Retrievers are smart, obedient, and eager to please. Hunters like their skill of bringing back ducks and other wild game. These dogs need a lot of exercise, and hunting is a great way to keep them in top shape.

sporting dog—a dog used to hunt game

Retrievers can be both hunting companions and beloved family members. Families love them because they are friendly and playful. Most retrievers have the perfect **temperament** for families with young children.

Retrievers bring back game both on land and in the water.

DOG FACT

Many retrievers work as guide dogs, police dogs, search and rescue dogs, or **therapy dogs**.

temperament—the combination of a dog's behavior and personality

therapy dog—a dog used to help people with emotional or physical challenges

BREEDS

In the United States, the most popular retriever breeds are the Labrador and the golden. The Chesapeake Bay retriever is also a popular choice of American dog owners. Other breeds include the curly-coated retriever, the flat-coated retriever, and the Nova Scotia duck tolling retriever. All of these dogs are strong and skilled hunting companions.

Labradors can be black, yellow, or brown.

DOG FACT

Labrador retrievers are called labs for short. Golden retrievers are nicknamed "goldens."

Golden retrievers are popular as family pets as well as hunting dogs.

The golden retriever breed began in Scotland in the 1800s. The Chesapeake Bay retriever was developed in the Chesapeake Bay area of Maryland. Four other retriever breeds developed in Canada. Labradors are from Newfoundland, where they were called St. John's Water Dogs. Both the curly-coated retriever and the flat-coated retriever are also believed to be from Newfoundland. As its name suggests, the Nova Scotia duck tolling retriever comes from Nova Scotia.

PERSONALITIES

All retrievers have the ability to bring game back to their owners. But each breed is a little different. The lab and the golden have easygoing personalities. Both have been among the most registered breeds with the American Kennel Club (AKC) for many years. These energetic dogs need plenty of exercise and playtime every day. They also must be trained not to jump up on people or chew shoes and other household objects.

Chesapeake Bays are strong water retrievers.

The Chesapeake Bay retriever is nicknamed the Chessie. Many people think it's the toughest water retriever. It will fetch birds out of even ice-cold waters. This intelligent dog needs firm, consistent rules and training.

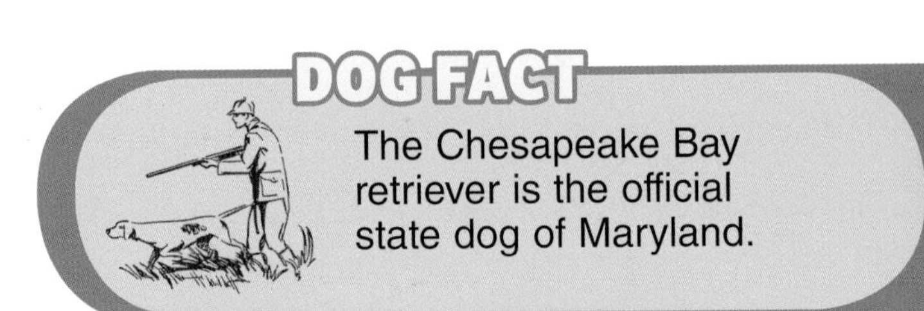

DOG FACT

The Chesapeake Bay retriever is the official state dog of Maryland.

The curly-coated retriever also eagerly dives into cold water. But it's best known for retrieving game in thick brush. Its thick, curly coat helps protect it from scratches. Curly-coated retrievers can be shy with strangers if owners don't **socialize** them well when they are young.

The flat-coated retriever becomes bored more easily than other retrievers. Their owners should keep training sessions fun, interesting, and short.

The Nova Scotia duck tolling retriever is called the toller. It is known for its loyalty. Its name comes from the Middle English word *toll*, meaning "**lure**."

socialize—to train to get along with people and other animals

lure—to attract something

Tolling Games

The Nova Scotia duck tolling retriever was bred to hunt birds near the water's edge. A hunt often involves a game between the dog and its owner. The hunter tosses a stick, which the dog fetches without barking.

As the hunter and the toller continue their quiet game, birds nearby move closer to get a better look. As soon as the birds are within range, the hunter fires the gun. The toller drops the stick and swims into the water to retrieve the fallen bird.

CHAPTER 2

PICK OF THE LITTER

Retrievers seem made for hunting. They are full of energy. Most love the water, and their thick coats repel moisture. Retrievers have strong, webbed feet and wide tails. Both features help make them powerful swimmers.

Retrievers also have "soft mouths," meaning they can carry birds without damaging them. This ability, along with their swimming skills, makes retrievers great duck hunters.

DOG FACT

The Nova Scotia duck tolling retriever is the smallest retriever breed. Some people mistake it for a small golden retriever.

CHOOSING A HUNTING RETRIEVER

Most hunters prefer to get their dogs as puppies. That way they can train the dog before it has had time to learn any bad habits. The best place to get a hunting dog is from a breeder who has a good reputation.

When choosing a breeder, do your homework first. You can ask breed organizations or hunting dog groups to refer you to a good breeder. When you contact the breeder, ask for references from people who have bought dogs from him or her.

Even puppies from the same litter can differ in temperament.

Make sure you visit the breeder's location. Ask to see where the dogs are kept and to meet the parents of the puppies. The kennel areas should be clean, and the puppies should be comfortable around people. Breeders can usually tell which pups will grow up to be the best hunters. Retrievers often show signs of **birdiness** when they are just a few weeks old. These signs include barking, tail wagging, and intently watching birds.

It's a good idea to meet your puppy's parents.

birdiness—natural talent for bird hunting

No matter where you live, many golden and Labrador breeders likely are located within a short distance. You can probably also find a Chesapeake Bay puppy fairly easily. But locating a Nova Scotia duck tolling retriever may be more difficult. Only about 500 are born each year in the United States. Check with breed organizations or rescue groups to find a toller puppy.

Labrador puppies are readily available.

RETRIEVER BREEDS

Breed	Height at shoulder	Weight	Personality	Life span
Chesapeake Bay retriever	21 to 26 inches (53 to 66 centimeters)	55 to 80 pounds (25 to 36 kilograms)	intelligent, loyal	11 to 13 years
Curly-coated retriever	23 to 27 inches (58 to 69 cm)	65 to 80 pounds (29 to 36 kg)	intelligent, sometimes shy	8 to 12 years
Flat-coated retriever	22 to 24.5 inches (56 to 62 cm)	60 to 70 pounds (27 to 32 kg)	intelligent, sociable	10 to 12 years
Golden retriever	21.5 to 24 inches (55 to 61 cm)	55 to 75 pounds (25 to 34 kg)	friendly, affectionate	10 to 12 years
Labrador retriever	21.5 to 24.5 inches (55 to 62 cm)	55 to 80 pounds (25 to 36 kg)	energetic, friendly	10 to 12 years
Nova Scotia duck tolling retriever	17 to 21 inches (43 to 53 cm)	37 to 51 pounds (17 to 23 kg)	playful, energetic	12 to 14 years

CHAPTER 3

LET THE TRAINING BEGIN

Training is important for any type of dog, but it is especially important for hunting breeds. No matter how birdy a puppy is, it won't become a good hunter on its own. You must take the time to help it develop retrieving skills. If you rush through training, your dog probably won't become the skilled hunter it could be.

You and your dog need to become a hunting team.

Training may seem like a difficult job. The good news is that it can be broken down into many smaller steps.

BEGINNING TRAINING

Begin training as soon as you take your retriever puppy home. Just like any pet, your puppy will need to learn a few basic commands. For example, your pup must learn how to sit, stay, and come to you. This basic training is the key to helping your retriever become a good hunting companion. If your dog doesn't obey you in the field, it could get hurt.

Start by teaching your dog basic commands.

Train your dog when it is a bit hungry. Your retriever will work harder to learn its commands if you use tasty treats as rewards. You can even use your dog's dinner as a reward. Just put the dry food in a bag and head to the backyard. Of course, you will want to reward your dog with praise as well.

When hunting, your dog will need to stay quiet and hidden from birds. If you plan to use a **blind** in the field, start by teaching your pup to use a crate. The two structures look a lot alike.

Crate training is one of the easiest things you will do with your dog. Simply place a treat inside the crate. When your pup goes inside to get it, tell your dog, "hide." Be sure to practice the hide command in the blind as well. With practice, your retriever will respond to the voice command without the treat.

Crate training (above) helps dogs learn to stay in a blind (right).

DOG FACT

When training or hunting, always take fresh water along for your dog and find some shade for regular breaks.

Training can take place in your own backyard.

Some owners prefer to train their dogs in their own backyards. Working one-on-one with your pet can keep both you and your dog focused. Other owners choose to attend a puppy training class with their dogs. The sights and sounds of a class may help your dog learn to ignore noise and other distractions while hunting.

blind—structure in which a hunter hides to shoot game

A dummy should be about the same size and weight as a bird.

HUNTER TRAINING

Once your puppy knows basic commands, move on to hunter training. This includes teaching your pup to retrieve **dummies**, which are also called bumpers. When your pup brings the dummy back to you, say, "give" as you gently take the dummy from its mouth. Then continue to throw the dummy. Soon your retriever will learn that "give" means to release the object in its mouth.

Don't teach your dog to retrieve balls or other toys. Doing so will only confuse it. Use bumpers whenever you play fetch together.

dummy—a training toy

Once your pup has the hang of retrieving, teach it to wait for your command before retrieving the dummy. This skill is important in the field. Use the "sit" and "stay" commands after you throw the dummy, holding your dog steady by the collar. Then release your dog as you say its name or "fetch." Your retriever will learn to wait for your command before going after a dummy or a bird.

Praise your retriever when it follows your commands.

MARKING

Before heading into the field with your retriever, practice **marking**. You can use a regular dummy, but scented bumpers or dead ducks often work better. Many hunters believe that marking can't be taught. They think a dog's marking skill depends on its birdiness. Either way, practice will only help your dog become better.

Some training dummies look like game birds.

marking—a dog's ability to find fallen game

When you start training your retriever to mark, throw the bumper or dummy where your dog can see it. Hold your dog steady as it focuses its sight on the dummy. Then say, "fetch" as you release the dog in the direction of the dummy. When your retriever picks up the dummy, use the "come" command to tell it to return to you. With practice, your dog will learn to retrieve birds that it doesn't see fall or that aren't clearly visible.

DOG FACT

Retrievers can hunt for as long as they are interested and able. Some dogs hunt for most of their lives.

The most valuable training tool you have is a positive attitude. Praise your dog for the things it does right. Punishing your pup for what it does wrong will only make your retriever afraid of you. Also, be patient. Just like people, dogs learn at different speeds.

CHAPTER 4

YOUR RETRIEVER AT HOME

Treat your retriever with kindness, and it will enjoy hunting with you for many years. Make your dog into a good hunting companion by building a strong relationship with it. A dog that trusts its owner is more likely to obey.

HAVING FUN

Retrievers need fun in their lives. Whatever you're doing, they'll want to be in the middle of the excitement. A trip to a lake is perfect. Just don't expect your retriever to stay at the cabin when it's time to go swimming! You probably won't make it into the water before your pet jumps in with all four paws.

Both timing and accuracy are tested in agility competitions.

Even when the weather isn't right for the dog paddle, your retriever will want to get out and play. Many owners enter their retrievers in dog shows, obedience competitions, and organized sports like **agility**. Retrievers are among the top champions in all these events.

agility—competitions in which dogs race through a series of obstacles

CARING FOR YOUR RETRIEVER

Owning a retriever isn't all fun and games. Like all dogs, retrievers need daily care. Your dog should eat nutritious food. Sharing junk food with your pet may make it happy, but it will hurt its health over time. The best dog foods are available at pet supply stores. You may want to choose a food made especially for active dogs.

Pups need to eat more often than adult dogs.

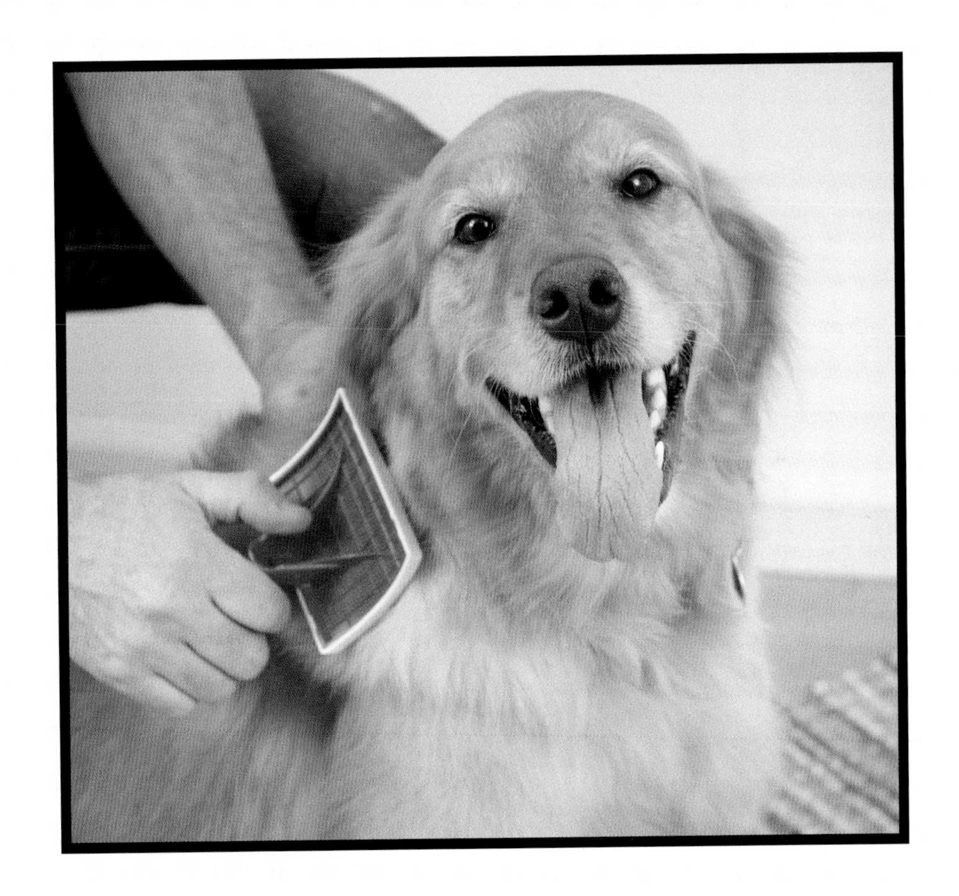

A retriever's coat isn't long enough to tangle, but it does shed. Brush your dog at least once a week. A retriever's skin has oils that help keep the dog's coat from holding water. Brushing helps release these oils. But bathing too often can strip them away. Limit your dog's baths to every month or two.

DOG FACT

The curly-coated retriever looks like it needs more grooming than other retrievers, but that isn't true. You won't need to brush or bathe this dog more often than any other retriever breed.

HEALTH ISSUES

Health problems are found in every dog breed. When you buy your dog, ask your breeder about health clearances. These tests show that your pup's parents have been checked for certain illnesses. A retriever breeder should have puppies checked for hip, elbow, and eye problems.

Your dog also needs to visit the veterinarian. Yearly checkups will help prevent some health problems and find others before they become too serious.

The vet will check your dog's health and give it needed vaccinations.

Hypothyroidism is a common illness in retrievers. Symptoms include weight gain without eating more, hair loss, and not wanting to exercise or play. Hypothyroidism can be treated with medicine, but finding it early is important. If left untreated, hypothyroidism can cause health problems such as liver and kidney disease.

Of all retrievers, goldens are most affected by cancer.

The worst disease that affects retrievers is cancer. It is the most common cause of death, especially for goldens. Check your dog for any unusual lumps or bumps whenever you brush it. You just might end up saving its life.

hypothyroidism—a condition caused by an underactive thyroid gland

Preventing Heartworm Disease

One of the biggest threats to your retriever's health is heartworm disease. Mosquitoes spread this common illness. It is almost impossible to keep mosquitoes from biting your dog in the field, but you can keep the insects from passing the disease to your dog. Ask your vet about giving your retriever a monthly heartworm preventative. Do this even if you live in an area where it is cold outside during hunting season. Mosquitoes can breed in temperatures as low as 57 degrees Fahrenheit (14 degrees Celsius). They can also be found wherever there is water—your retriever's favorite place.

DOG FACT

Dogs are naturally most active at dawn and dusk. They often sleep during mid-day.

Retrievers are loving and loyal companions, both on the hunt and at home. If you treat your dog well, you will end up with both a talented hunting buddy and a faithful friend.

GLOSSARY

agility (uh-GI-luh-tee)—competitions in which dogs race through a series of obstacles

birdiness (BURD-ee-nuhss)—a dog's natural talent for bird hunting

blind (BLYND)—a structure in which a hunter hides to shoot game

dummy (DUHM-ee)—a training toy used as a substitute for a bird

hypothyroidism (hye-puh-THY-roy-diz-uhm)—a medical condition caused by an underactive thyroid gland

lure (LOOR)—to attract something

marking (MAHR-king)—a hunting dog's ability to find fallen game

socialize (SOH-shuh-lize)—to train to get along with people and other animals

sporting dog (SPORT-ing DAWG)—a dog used to hunt game

therapy dog (THARE-uh-pee DAWG)—a dog used to help people with emotional or physical challenges

temperament (TEM-pur-uh-muhnt)—the combination of a dog's behavior and personality; the way an animal usually acts or responds to situations shows its temperament

READ MORE

Larrew, Brekka Hervey. *Labrador Retrievers*. All About Dogs. Mankato, Minn.: Capstone Press, 2009.

Loveland, Cherylon. *Retriever Puppy Training: The Right Start for Hunting*. Crawford, Colo.: Alpine Publications, 2010.

Omoth, Tyler. *Duck Hunting for Kids.* Into the Great Outdoors. North Mankato, Minn.: Capstone Press, 2013.

Pound, Blake. *Pheasant Hunting.* Pilot Books: Outdoor Adventures. Minneapolis: Bellwether Media, Inc., 2013.

INTERNET SITES

FactHound offers a safe, fun way to find Internet sites related to this book. All of the sites on FactHound have been researched by our staff.

Here's all you do:

Visit *www.facthound.com*

Type in this code: 9781429699099

Check out projects, games and lots more at **www.capstonekids.com**

INDEX